The Tapping Tale

Judy Giglio
Illustrated by Joe Cepeda

Green Light Readers
Harcourt, Inc.
San Diego   New York   London

First Green Light Readers edition 2000
Green Light Readers is a registered trademark of Harcourt, Inc.

Library of Congress Cataloging-in-Publication Data
Giglio, Judy.
The tapping tale/Judy Giglio; illustrated by Joe Cepeda.
—1st Green Light Readers ed.
p. cm.
"Green Light Readers."
Summary: On her first sleepover, a mysterious tapping sound keeps Ronda awake.
[1. Sleepovers—Fiction. 2. Dogs—Fiction.] I. Cepeda, Joe, ill. II. Title.
PZ7.G366Tap 2000
[E]—dc21   99-6808
ISBN 0-15-202572-3
ISBN 0-15-202578-2 (pb)

A C E G H F D B

A C E G H F D B (pb)

Printed in Mexico.

Pat ran to see Ronda.

At last, Ronda was spending the night!

"Mom, Ronda is here."

Pat and Ronda played all day.

At last, it was time to sleep.

It was dark in Pat's room.

"What's that tapping?" asked Ronda.

"I can look in the hall," said Pat.

"Look!" said Ronda. "This is what's tapping."

"I think it's a tail!" said Ronda.

"Oh, that's Rip!" said Pat. "Rip,
hop up here."

"Rip is happy to see you," said Pat.

"Oh, Rip," said Ronda. "This is better. You can sleep up here!"

Meet the Illustrator

Joe Cepeda reads a story many times before he works on the pictures for it. He doesn't start drawing until he knows the story well. First he draws the place where the story happens. He draws the people last. He likes to make the characters look like people he really knows!